CHARMING
THE
HIGHLANDER

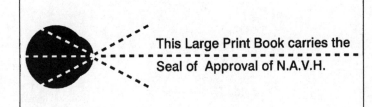

This Large Print Book carries the
Seal of Approval of N.A.V.H.

CHARMING
THE
HIGHLANDER

JANET
CHAPMAN

Thorndike Press • Waterville, Maine

Published in 2005 by arrangement with
Pocket Books, an imprint of Simon & Schuster, Inc.

Thorndike Press® Large Print Romance.

The tree indicium is a trademark of Thorndike Press.

The text of this Large Print edition is unabridged.
Other aspects of the book may vary from the original edition.

Set in 16 pt. Plantin by Ramona Watson.

Printed in the United States on permanent paper.

Library of Congress Cataloging-in-Publication Data

Chapman, Janet.
    Charming the highlander / by Janet Chapman.
      p. cm. — (Thorndike Press large print romance)
    ISBN 0-7862-7548-0 (lg. print : hc : alk. paper)
    1. Survival after airplane accidents, shipwrecks, etc. —
Fiction. 2. Scots — United States — Fiction. 3. Women
scientists — Fiction. 4. Time travel — Fiction. 5. Maine
— Fiction. 6. Large type books. I. Title. II. Thorndike
Press large print romance series.
PS3603.H372C48 2005
  813'.6—dc22   2005000805

THIS ONE IS FOR ROBBIE,

who stood guard at the gate all these years,
refusing to let the world intrude
on my dream.

For your patience, support, and strength to
shoulder the load, for being a rock through
the currents of life — quite simply put,
thank you.

It's been twenty-five years, husband, and
the journey only gets better.

As the Founder/CEO of NAVH, the only national health agency solely devoted to those who, although not totally blind, have an eye disease which could lead to serious visual impairment, I am pleased to recognize Thorndike Press* as one of the leading publishers in the large print field.

Founded in 1954 in San Francisco to prepare large print textbooks for partially seeing children, NAVH became the pioneer and standard setting agency in the preparation of large type.

Today, those publishers who meet our standards carry the prestigious "Seal of Approval" indicating high quality large print. We are delighted that Thorndike Press is one of the publishers whose titles meet these standards. We are also pleased to recognize the significant contribution Thorndike Press is making in this important and growing field.

Lorraine H. Marchi, L.H.D.
Founder/CEO
NAVH

* Thorndike Press encompasses the following imprints: Thorndike, Wheeler, Walker and Large Print Press.

Prologue

The Highlands of Scotland, A.D. 1200

It was a hellish day to be casting a spell. The relentless glare of the sun nearing its zenith reflected off the parched landscape in waves of stifling heat. Occasional dust devils, pushed into action by an arid breeze, were the only movement in the gleann below. Even the birds refused to stir from the protective shade of the thirsty oak forest.

Leaning heavily on his ancient cherrywood staff for support, Pendaär slowly picked his way to the top of the bluff, silently scolding himself for making the climb in full ceremonial dress. More than once the aging wizard had to stop and free his robe when it snagged on a bush.

God's teeth, but he was tired.

Pendaär stopped and leaned against a boulder to catch his breath, pushing his now damp, long white hair from his face as he searched the road below for any sign of the MacKeages. Thank the stars, he'd soon be leaving this godforsaken place. He'd had his fill of this harsh time, of the constant struggle for survival, and of the incessant, senseless wars between arrogant men fighting for power and position.

Yes, he was more than ready to discover the comforts of a much more modern world.

Pendaär shook his robes and brushed at the dust gathering near the hem, once again cursing the heavenly bodies for marching into perfect alignment on such a god-awful day. But Laird Greylen MacKeage was about to begin a most remarkable journey, and Pendaär was determined to have a good seat for the send-off. Anxious to get into position, the tired wizard pushed away from his resting place and continued up the hill.

Once he finally reached the summit, he settled himself on an outcropping of granite and lifted his face to the sun, letting the warm breeze rustle his hair and cool his neck. When he was finally able to breathe without panting, Pendaär brought his gnarled cherrywood staff to his lap and fingered the burls in the wood, slowly repeating the words of his spell, concentrating on reciting them correctly.

Thirty-one years of painstaking work

was culminating today. Thirty-one years of watching over and worrying about the powerful, oftentimes hell-raising laird of the clan MacKeage was finally coming to fruition. The sun had nearly reached its zenith. The celestial bodies were falling into alignment.

And Greylen MacKeage was late.

Pendaär wasn't surprised. The boy had been late for his own birth by a good two weeks. And now he was in danger of missing the very destiny the stars had promised thirty-two years ago, on the night of the young laird's conception.

Greylen MacKeage carried the seed of Pendaär's successor.

Greylen's match, however, had been born in twentieth-century America. And getting the two of them together was causing the aging wizard untold fits of frustration.

It would help, of course, if he knew who the woman was.

And that was the problem. The powers-that-be had a heartless and sometimes warped sense of humor, giving Pendaär the choice of knowing only the man or the woman who would beget his heir, but not both.

Pendaär had chosen the spell that would

9

show him Greylen MacKeage. Then he had spent the first thirty-one years of Greylen's life trying to keep him alive. It had not been an easy task. The MacKeages were a small but mighty clan who seemed to have more enemies than most. They were constantly at war with one tribe or another, and their brash young laird insisted on riding up front into battle.

But it was the woman Pendaär wished to know more about now. Was she beautiful? Intelligent? Did she have the spunk and the courage necessary to match up with a man like Greylen MacKeage? Surely the other half of this magical couple would have what it takes to give birth to a wizard. Wouldn't she?

Pendaär had spent many sleepless nights with such worries. He had even gone so far as to visit the northwestern mountains of Maine, eight hundred years into the future, in hopes of recognizing the woman. But the spell that protected her was sealed, and no magic he possessed would unlock it.

Only the man destined to have her could find her. In his own way and on his own terms, only Greylen MacKeage could claim the woman the ancients had chosen as his mate.

If, that is, he ever showed up.

Nearly an hour passed before Greylen and three of his warriors rounded the bend in the rutted path and finally came into sight. And what a sight they were. The MacKeages rode in silence, single file, on powerful warhorses they controlled with seemingly little effort. The men were dirty, and maybe a bit tired from their long journey, but they appeared to have made the trip without mishap.

Pendaär scrambled to his feet. It was time. He pushed back the sleeves of his gown and pointed his staff at the sky, closing his eyes as he began to chant the spell that would call forth the powers of nature.

A battle cry suddenly pierced the air.

Greylen MacKeage brought his warhorse to a halt and pulled his sword free of its sheath at the sound, seeing the mounted warriors rushing toward him from the cover of the trees. They were masked in war paint, in full battle dress, their swords held high as they descended upon Greylen and his small band of travelers.

It was the MacBains, the ambushing bastards.

Greylen's brother, Morgan, immediately moved to his side, and Grey's other two men quickly flanked them to form an imposing wall of might. Greylen looked first to his right and then to his left before returning his attention to his enemy and, with a grin of anticipation, raised his sword and answered the call to battle with a shout of his own. Spurring their horses forward, the four MacKeage warriors charged the MacBains, their laughter quickly lost in the sounds of battle.

Greylen had not sought out this fight, but, by God, if Michael MacBain wanted to die today, Grey would be kind enough to help the blackheart to hell.

If, that is, he could keep Ian from dispatching the bastard first. A good five years past his prime, Ian MacKeage was fighting like a man possessed, and it was all Greylen could do to guard his old friend's back while protecting his own. The smell of horse sweat rose with the dust kicked up by the battle; the taste of blood, bile, and anger burned at the back of Greylen's throat.

His horse stumbled from the charge of MacBain's horse, and Grey ducked to the right and swung his arm in an arc, striking Michael MacBain square on the back with the flat of his sword. The blow would have unseated a lesser man, but MacBain merely laughed out loud and turned his horse away.

This battle was an exercise in futility, and both men knew it. Six MacBains to four MacKeages was hardly fair. It would take another half dozen MacBains to even the fight, and Greylen wondered again at Michael's intent today.

Was the young man only looking for sport? Maybe pricking Greylen's anger? Or had he grown tired of waiting for Grey's retaliation?

Aye. Michael was weary of watching his back these last three years and was now trying to force a war that Greylen had no intention of declaring. No one woman, no matter how innocent and long dead, was worth an entire clan rising in arms against another. Michael need not die today to feel damnation's fires. Greylen would bet his sword arm that MacBain was already well acquainted with Hades.

A brilliant flash of light high on the hill caught Greylen's attention, and he pivoted his warhorse to get a better view. A lone figure stood on the bluff, full robes billowing in the rising wind, tangled white hair obscuring his face. His arms were outstretched, raised against a darkening sky, one hand holding a stick that glowed like the coals of a long-burning fire.

Grey darted a quick look back at the

battle and saw Michael MacBain suddenly pull his own horse to a stop and look toward the bluff. But before Grey could dwell on what he was seeing, he and MacBain were both pulled back into the battle that Grey suddenly had no desire to fight.

Pendaär closed his eyes and loudly chanted the spell of his ancestors. Lightning crackled around him, lifting his hair from his neck as the wind molded his robes to his legs. Light burned from beneath his eyelids, and the old wizard staggered under the assault.

The sounds of the battle below rose louder.

Pendaär slowly opened his eyes and glared at the weathered, burl-knotted staff in his hand. Nothing had happened. He looked back at the gleann. Those lawless MacBains were still plaguing the MacKeages.

He raised his staff again and commanded the clouds to boil, the winds to howl, and the rains to fall. He reached deep within his soul and summoned the power of the ancients, adding their strength to his own fourteen hundred years of wizardry. Greylen MacKeage must not be harmed this day. He had a much more

14

noble destiny, one that would take him on a journey the likes of which few mortal men had known.

With his legs spread wide and his feet planted firmly on the bluff, Pendaär braced himself for the familiar jolt of energy he was about to release. His head raised and his arms outstretched, he spoke his wizard's language more slowly to cast his spell of time over matter. His long white hair became charged with electricity once again, and every muscle in his body trembled with power.

And still nothing happened.

With a mighty roar of frustration, Pendaär hurled the cherrywood rod at the boulder he had been sitting on. The staff bounced once and crackled to life before it was suddenly grabbed by a bolt of lightning. It floated high over the gleann, arcs of energy shooting from it in every direction.

A great darkness descended over the land. The clash of steel, shouts of men, and pounding of giant hooves gave way to deafening booms of thunder. A torrential rain poured down, casting a sheet of confusion over the chaos. Trees bent until they snapped. Boulders split, and rocks tumbled free from the bluff where Pendaär stood.

And Pendaär fell with them, rolling head over feet, his now soaked robes tangling around him as he struggled to find purchase on the rockslide. Rain and mud and rocks and shrubs crashed down the side of the bluff, pulling the wizard with them.

And when the turmoil finally ceased, Pendaär landed with a jarring thud, faceup in a puddle of mud. The sun returned, beating down on his face with enough strength to make him squint.

But it was the silence that finally made him stir. The old wizard slowly sat up and pushed the hair from his face, looking around. Then he rubbed his eyes with his fists and looked again, before burying his head in his hands with a groan of dismay.

What had he done?

Yes, Greylen MacKeage had certainly begun his journey this day, but it seemed the warrior did not travel alone.

Because not one MacKeage remained to continue the fight. Not one of the ambushing MacBains could be seen. Even their horses had disappeared with the storm. Naught was left of the battle but trodden mud, churned grass, and the fading rumble of distant thunder.

Pendaär gaped at the empty gleann.

He hadn't gone with them.

Greylen MacKeage, his men, and those damned MacBains had traveled through time without him. God's teeth! They were in the twenty-first century without direction or purpose, and he was sitting here like a wart on a toad, having no idea where his contrary staff had run off to.

Pendaär scrambled to his feet and began to search for it, wringing his hands and muttering curses as he ran frantically in circles. He needed to be with the warriors. He needed to see that they didn't kill each other, or kill some innocent twenty-first-century person who might unwittingly stumble upon them.

Pendaär searched for half an hour before finding his staff. It was standing upright in a puddle of mud, still quivering with volatile energy. The wizard lifted his robes and stepped into the puddle, grasping the humming staff and tugging, trying to free it. The cherrywood hissed and violently twisted, apparently still angry at being thrown away.

Pendaär ignored its grumbling, giving it a mighty tug that sent him sprawling backward onto the wet ground. He clutched the staff to his chest and muttered a prayer for patience.

It took the wizard another twenty minutes to soothe the disgruntled cherrywood, running his hands gently over the burls as he whispered his apologies.

The staff slowly calmed, and Pendaär finally stood up. He urged the cherrywood to grow again, to draw the powers of the universe back to his hand. The staff lengthened and warmed and hummed, this time with cooperation.

Pendaär closed his eyes and began to chant a new spell as he waved the staff in a reaching arc. A satchel suddenly appeared at his feet, and Pendaär's wet and muddy robe magically disappeared from his body. He opened his eyes, smoothed down the crisp, black wool cassock he was now wearing, and fingered the white collar at his throat.

Pendaär smiled. Aye. That was better. He was once again in command of his magic.

He quickly knelt and opened the satchel to make sure everything he needed for his own journey was there. He pushed aside the rosary beads, toothbrush, and electric clippers he was anxious to try, feeling instead for the bundles of paper money he had asked for. They were sitting just beneath another wool cassock, five pairs of socks, and a heavy red plaid Mackinaw coat.

Everything seemed to be in place.

Pendaär straightened and lifted his staff to the sky, chanting again his spell to move matter through time. Darkness returned to the gleann, lightning flashed through the heavens, and Pendaär clutched his satchel, closed his eyes, and hunched his shoulders against the chaos about to consume him.

Dancing sparks swirled around him with ever increasing speed, charged by electricity that made the air crackle with blinding white light. The old wizard took one last peek at the twelfth-century landscape before it disappeared, his laughter trailing to echoes as he excitedly set out on his own remarkable journey to help Greylen MacKeage find the woman he was destined to claim.

Chapter One

Early winter in modern-day America

It was sheer stubbornness keeping Mary Sutter alive now. She still had something she needed to say, and she refused to give in to the lure of death until she was done giving her instructions to her sister, Grace.

Grace sat by the hospital bed, her eyes swollen with unshed tears and her heart breaking as she watched Mary struggle to speak. The gentle beeps and soft hums were gone; the countless medical machines monitoring her decline had been removed just an hour ago. A pregnant stillness had settled over the room in their stead. Grace sat in painful silence, willing her sister to live.

The phone call telling Grace of the automobile accident had come at noon yesterday. By the time she had arrived at the hospital, Mary's child had already been born, taken from his mother by emergency surgery. And by six this morning, the doctors had finally conceded that her sister was dying.

Younger by three years, Mary had always been the more practical of the two sisters, the down-to-earth one. She'd also been the bossier of the two girls. By the time she was five, Mary had been ruling the Sutter household by imposing her will on their aging parents, her older half brothers still living at home, and Grace. And when their parents had died nine years ago in a boating accident, it had been eighteen-year-old Mary who had handled the tragedy. Their six half brothers had come home from all four corners of the world, only to be told their only chore was that of pallbearers to their father and stepmother.

After the beautiful but painful ceremony, the six brothers had returned to their families and jobs, Grace had gone back to Boston to finish her doctorate in mathematical physics, and Mary had stayed in Pine Creek, Maine, claiming the aged Sutter homestead as her own.

Which was why, when Mary had shown up on her doorstep in Norfolk, Virginia, four months ago, Grace had been truly surprised. It would take something mighty powerful to roust her sister out of the woods she loved so much. But Mary only had to take off her jacket for Grace to understand.

Her sister was pregnant. Mary was just beginning to show when she had arrived, and it was immediately obvious to Grace that her sister didn't know what to do about the situation.

They'd had several discussions over the last four months, some of them heated. But Mary, being the stubborn woman she was, refused to talk about the problem with Grace. She was there to gather her thoughts and her courage and decide what to do. Yes, she loved the baby's father more than life itself, but no, she wasn't sure she could marry him.

Was he married to someone else? Grace had wanted to know.

No.

Did he live in the city, then? She'd have to move?

No.

Was he a convicted felon?

Of course not.

For the life of her, Grace could not get her sister to tell her why she couldn't go home and set a wedding date — hopefully before the birth date.

Mary wouldn't even tell her the man's name. She was closed-mouthed about everything except for the fact that he was a Scot and that he had arrived in Pine Creek just last year. They had met at a grange supper and had fallen madly in love over the next three months. She'd gotten pregnant the first time they made love.

It was another four months of bliss, and then Mary's world had suddenly careened out of control. In the quiet evening hours during a walk one day, the Scot had told her a fantastical tale (Mary's words), and then he had asked her to marry him.

Two days later Mary had arrived at Grace's home in Virginia.

And for the last four months, Grace had asked Mary to reveal what the Scot had told her, but her sister had remained silent and brooding. Until she had announced yesterday, out of the blue and with a promise to explain everything later, that she was returning to Pine Creek. Only she hadn't been gone an hour when the phone call came. Mary had not even made it out of the city when her car had been pushed into the opposite lane of a six-lane highway by a drunk driver. It had taken the rescue team three hours to free Mary from what was left of her rental car.

And now she was dying.

And her new baby son was just down the

hall, surprisingly healthy for having been pulled from the sanctuary of his mother's womb a whole month early.

A nurse entered the room and checked the IV hooked up to Mary, then left just as silently, leaving Grace with only a sympathetic smile and a whisper that Grace should let her know if she needed anything. Grace rushed to follow her out the door.

"Can she see the baby?" Grace asked the nurse. "Can she hold him?"

The nurse contemplated the request for only a second. Her motherly face suddenly brightened. "I think I can arrange it," she said, nodding her approval. "Yes, I think we should get that baby in his mother's arms as soon as possible."

She laid a gentle hand on Grace's shoulder. "I'm sorry, Miss Sutter, for what's happening here. But the accident did a lot of damage to your sister, and the emergency cesarean complicated things. Your sister's spleen was severely ruptured, and now her organs are shutting down one at a time. She just isn't responding to anything we try. It's a wonder she's even conscious."

The nurse leaned in and said in a whisper, as if they were in church,

"They're calling him the miracle baby, you know. Not one scratch on his beautiful little body. And he's not even needing an incubator, although they have him in one as a precaution."

Grace smiled back, but it was forced. "Please bring Mary her son," she said. "It's important she sees that he's okay. She's been asking about him."

With that said, Grace returned to the room to find Mary awake. Her sister's sunken blue gaze followed her as she rounded the bed and sat down beside her again.

"I want a promise," Mary said in a labored whisper.

Grace carefully picked up Mary's IV-entangled hand and held it. "Anything," she told her, giving her fingers a gentle squeeze. "Just name it."

Mary smiled weakly. "Now I know I'm dying," she said, trying to squeeze back. "You were eight the last time you promised me anything without knowing the facts first."

Grace made a production of rolling her eyes at her sister, not letting her see how much that one simple word, *dying,* wounded her heart. She didn't want her sister to die. She wanted to go back just two days, to when they were arguing the way sisters did when they loved each other. "And I'll probably regret this promise just as much," Grace told her with false cheerfulness.

Mary's eyes darkened. "Yes, you probably will."

"Tell me," she told her sister.

"I want you to promise to take my baby home to his father."

Grace was stunned. She was expecting Mary to ask her to raise her son, not give him away.

"Take him to his father?" Grace repeated, slowly shaking her head. "The same man you ran away from four months ago?"

Mary weakly tightened her grip on Grace's hand. "I was running back to him yesterday," she reminded her.

"I'm not making any promises until you tell me why you left Pine Creek in the first place. And what made you decide to return," Grace told her. "Tell me what scared you badly enough to leave."

Mary stared blankly at nothing, and for a moment Grace was afraid she had lost consciousness. Mary's breathing came in short, shallow breaths that were slowly growing more labored. Her eyelids were heavy, her pupils glazed and distant. Grace feared her question had fallen on deaf ears. But then Mary quietly began to speak.

"He scared me," she said. "When he told me his story, he scared the daylights out of me."

"What story?" Grace asked, reaching for Mary's hand again. "What did he tell you?"

Mary's eyes suddenly brightened with a spark of mischief. "Lift my bed," she instructed. "I want to see the look on your face, my scientist sister, when you hear what he told me."

Grace pushed the bed's lift button and watched her sister sit up. Mary never called her a scientist unless she had some outrageous idea she wanted to convince her was possible. Grace was the rocket scientist, Mary was the dreamer.

"Okay. Out with it," she demanded, seizing on that one little spark like a lifeline. She settled a pillow behind Mary's head. "What did lover boy tell you that made you run away?"

"His name is Michael."

"Finally. The man has a name. Michael what?"

Mary didn't answer. She was already focused on gathering her words as she stared off into space over Grace's right shoulder.

"He moved to Pine Creek from Nova Scotia," Mary said. "And before that he lived in Scotland." She turned her gaze to Grace, her drug-dilated, blue eyes suddenly looking apprehensive. "He told me he was born in Scotland." And then, in a near whisper, she added, "In the year 1171."

Grace straightened in her chair and stared at Mary. "What?" she whispered back, convinced she had heard wrong. "When?"

"In 1171."

"You're meaning in November of 1971, right?"

Mary slowly shook her head. "No. The year eleven hundred seventy-one. Eight hundred years ago."

Grace thought about that. *Fantastical* was putting it mildly. But then she suddenly laughed softly. "Mary. You ran away from the man because he believes in reincarnation?" She waved her hand in the air. "Heck, half the population of the world believes they've led past lives. There are whole religions based on reincarnation."

"No," Mary insisted, shaking her head. "That's not what Michael meant. He says he spent the first twenty-five years of his life in twelfth-century Scotland and the last four years here in modern-day North America. That a storm carried him through time."

Grace was at a loss for words.

"Actually," Mary continued, "five of his clan and their warhorses came with him."

Grace sucked in her breath at the sorrow in her sister's eyes. "And where are these men now? And their . . . their . . . horses?"

"They're dead," Mary said. "All of them. Michael's the last of his clan." Her features suddenly relaxed. "Except for his son now."

She reached for Grace's hand and gripped it with surprising strength. "That's why I was going back. Family is important to Michael. He's all alone in this world, except for our baby. And that's why you have to take his son to him."

Mary let out a tired breath. "I'm dying." She looked at Grace with sadly resigned eyes. "You have to do this for me, Gracie. And you have to tell Michael I love him." Tears were spilling over her cheeks.

Grace stared down at her sister through tears of her own.

"Will you listen to yourself, Mare? You're asking me to take your son to a madman. If he really believes he's traveled through time, then he's touched in the head. You want him bringing up your child?"

Mary released a shuddering breath and closed her eyes again. A stillness settled over the room once more.

Mary was asking her to take a child — her nephew — to a man who was not sane. Grace covered her face with her hands. How could Mary ask such a thing of her?

And how could she not grant her sister's dying wish?

The door opened again with a muted whoosh, and Grace looked up to see a clear plastic basinet being wheeled into the room. White cotton-covered little arms waved in the air, the sleeves so long there was no sign of the tiny hands that should be sticking out of the ends.

Grace had to wipe the tears from her eyes to see that Mary was awake again, straining to see her baby.

"Oh, God. Look at him, Gracie," Mary whispered, reaching toward him with a shaking hand. "He's so tiny."

The nurse placed the basinet next to the bed. She put a pillow on Mary's lap and carefully placed Mary's cast-covered right arm on top of it. Then she picked up the tiny, squeaking bundle from the basinet and gently settled him on the pillow in Mary's lap.

"He's so pink," Mary said, gently cupping his head. "And so beautiful."

"He's thinking it's dinnertime," the nurse said. "You might as well feed him a bit of sugar water if you feel up to it."

"Oh, yes," Mary said, already tugging at his blanket.

The nurse repositioned him in the crook of Mary's broken arm and handed her a tiny bottle of clear liquid with a nipple on it. The tubes sticking in Mary's left hand tangled in her child's kicking feet. The nurse moved around the bed, handed the bottle to Grace, and carefully removed the IV from Mary's hand, covering it with a bandage she pulled from her smock.

"There. You don't really need this," she said, hanging the tubes on the IV stand. She took the bottle of sugar water back and stuck it in the fretting baby's mouth. Free now, Mary awkwardly but eagerly took over.

The nurse watched for a minute, making sure Mary could handle the chore, then turned to Grace.

"I'm going to leave you in privacy," the nurse said, her eyes betraying her sadness as she smiled at Mary and her son. She looked back at Grace. "Just ring for me if you need anything. I'll come immediately."

Panic immobilized Grace. The nurse was leaving them alone? Neither one of them knew a thing about babies.

"Look, Gracie. Isn't he beautiful?" Mary asked.

Grace stood up and examined her nephew. Beautiful? He was unquestionably the homeliest baby she had ever seen. His puffy cheeks were red with exertion, his eyes were scrunched closed, his chin and neck blended into a series of overlapping wrinkles, and gobs of dark straight hair shot out from under a bright blue knit cap.

"He's gorgeous," she told Mary.

"Pull off his cap," her sister asked. "I want to see his hair."

Grace gently eased off her nephew's cap but was immediately tempted to slip it back on. Two rather large, perfectly formed ears popped out a good inch from his head, pushing his now freed hair into frenzied spikes.

He looked like a troll.

"Isn't he beautiful?" Mary repeated.

"He's gorgeous," Grace reconfirmed, trying with all her might to see her nephew the way her sister did.

Mary was the animal lover in the Sutter

household and was forever dragging home scruffy kittens, wounded birds and chipmunks, and mangy dogs. It was no wonder Mary thought her little son was precious.

He was. Homely, but precious.

"Let's undress him," Mary said. "Help me count his fingers and toes."

Startled, Grace looked at her sister. "Count them? Why? Do you think he's missing some?"

Mary gave a weak laugh as she wiped her son's mouth with the edge of his blanket. "Of course not. That's just what new mothers do."

Grace decided to humor her sister. Gingerly, she attempted to undo the strings at the bottom of the tiny nightshirt. It was a difficult task as the baby, now happy with a full belly, kept kicking his legs as he mouthed giant bubbles from his pursed lips.

Finally, with her two good hands and Mary's unsteady uninjured one, they freed his legs. Grace held up first one foot and then the other and counted his toes out loud.

She counted them again.

Twelve.

Six on each tiny foot.

Mary gave a weak shriek of joy. At least,

it sounded joyful. Grace stared at her numbly.

"Gifts from his daddy," Mary said in a winded whisper. "Michael has six toes on each foot."

And this was a joyful thing? Grace wanted to ask. Being deformed was good?

"Pull his shirt and diaper off," Mary said then. "I want to see him naked."

Grace was afraid to. What other surprises was the clothing hiding? But she did as her sister asked, even though she feared the tiny baby would break from her handling. She didn't know what she was doing. Heck, she hadn't even played with dolls when she was a kid. She had hiked and fished with her father until she was eight, until one of her older brothers had brought home a biography of Albert Einstein and she had discovered the world of science. From then on it was telescopes, science books, and mathematical formulas written on chalkboards.

Grace took off the baby's nightshirt and peeled off the diaper. She gasped and quickly covered him back up.

Mary pulled the diaper completely off. "You're a prude, Gracie," Mary said, cupping her baby's bottom. "He's supposed to look like that. He'll grow into it." Mary

traced the outline of his face, then posses-
sively rubbed her fingers over his entire
body. "Get a new diaper before we get
sprayed," she said.

Grace quickly complied. And between
the two of them and their three hands, they
eventually got him changed and back into
his nightshirt.

Grace was just retying the strings at his
feet when she noticed a tear fall onto her
hand. She stopped and looked up to find
Mary silently crying as she stared down at
her son.

"What's the matter, Mare? Are you in
pain?" she asked, holding the baby's feet so
they couldn't kick out and hurt her.

Mary slowly shook her head, never
taking her eyes off her son as she ran a
finger over his cheek again. "I want to see
him grow up," she whispered in a voice
that was growing more fatigued, more
faint, by the minute. She looked at Grace.
"I want to be there for him when he falls
and skins his knee, catches his first snake,
kisses his first girl, and gets his heart
broken every other day."

Grace flinched as if she'd been struck.
She closed her eyes against the pain that
welled up in her throat, forcing herself not
to cry.

Mary reached up and rubbed her trembling finger over Grace's cheek, just as she had done to her son's. "So it's up to you, Gracie. You have to be there for him, for me. Take him to his daddy, and be there for both of them. Promise me?"

"He's not sane, Mary. He thinks he traveled through time."

Mary looked back at her son. "Maybe he did."

Grace wanted to scream. Were the drugs in her sister's body clouding her judgment? Was she so fatigued, so mentally weakened, that she didn't realize what she was asking?

"Mary," she said, taking her sister by the chin and making her look at her. "People can't travel through time."

"I don't care if he came from Mars, Gracie. I love him. And he will love our son more than anyone else can. They need each other, and I need your promise to bring them together."

Grace walked away from the bed to look out the window. She was loath to grant such a promise. She didn't know a thing about babies, but she was intelligent and financially stable. How hard could it be to raise one little boy? She could read books on child-rearing and promise him a good life with lots of love and attention.

She had never met this Michael the Scot, and she sure as heck didn't like what she did know about him.

But then, she was even more reluctant to deny Mary her wish. This was the first time her sister had ever asked anything of her, and she was torn between her love for Mary and her worry for her nephew.

"Come get in bed with us, Gracie," Mary said. "Just like we used to."

Grace turned around to find Mary with her eyes closed and her child clutched tightly to her chest. The infant was sleeping. Grace returned to the bed and quickly lowered it. Without hesitation she kicked off her shoes, lowered the side bar, and climbed up beside her sister. Mary immediately snuggled against her.

"Ummm. This is nice," Mary murmured, not opening her eyes. "When was the last time we shared a bed?"

"Mom and Dad's funeral," Grace reminded her. She laid her hand on the baby's backside which was sticking up in the air. "Don't you think we should give this guy a name?" she asked, rubbing his back.

"No. That's Michael's privilege," Mary said. "Until then, just call him Baby."

"Baby what? You didn't tell me his father's last name."

"It's MacBain. Michael MacBain. He bought the Bigelow Christmas Tree Farm."

That was news to Grace. "What happened to John and Ellen Bigelow?"

"They still live there. Michael moved in with them," Mary said, her voice growing distant. She turned and looked at Grace, her once beautiful, vibrant blue eyes now glazed with lackluster tears. "He's a good man, Gracie. As solid as a rock," she said, closing her eyes again.

Except he believes he's eight hundred years old, Grace thought. She moved her hand from her nephew's bottom to her sister's hair, brushing it away from her forehead.

"I'm still waiting for your promise," Mary said, turning her face into Grace's palm.

Grace took a deep breath and finally spoke the words she had so stubbornly, and maybe selfishly, been avoiding.

"I promise, Mare. I'll take your son to Michael MacBain."

Mary kissed Grace's palm and sighed deeply, settling comfortably closer. "And you'll scatter my ashes on TarStone Mountain," she said then, her voice trailing off to a whisper. "On Summer Solstice morning."

"On . . . on Summer Solstice. I promise."

Grace left one hand cupping Mary's head and the other one cradling Baby as a patient, gentle peace returned to the room. Grace placed herself in the crook of her sister's shoulder, feeling the weakening drum of life beneath her tear-dampened cheek.

In two hours it was over, without the pain of a struggle. Mary's heart simply stopped beating. The only sound that remained was the soft, gentle breathing of a sleeping baby.

Chapter Two

If lies were raindrops, Grace would surely be in danger of drowning. She had told so many untruths and prevarications these last four weeks, she barely remembered half of them. And those she did remember were threatening to come back and bite her on the backside.

Grace closed the last of her suitcases and snapped the lock into place. Then she went hunting for her carry-on bag. Twice she had to push her way past Jonathan, and twice he ignored the fact that she wasn't interested in what he was saying.

Or, rather, what he was demanding.

Jonathan Stanhope III was the owner and CEO of StarShip Spaceline, a high-tech company intent on making space travel for private citizens a reality in the very near future. Employing nearly three hundred people, StarShip was on the cutting edge of scientific discovery, and Jonathan had been Grace's boss for the last eighteen months.

He was also the man she hoped to marry.

Although at the moment she wished he would climb aboard one of their untested shuttles and shoot himself into space.

Jonathan was not pleased that she was leaving. He'd done his boss's duty and given her four weeks to "get over" her sister's death, and he couldn't believe that she'd had the audacity to expect even more time.

"But you're talking about *Maine*, Grace," he said for the fourteenth time, following her out of the bedroom and into the kitchen. "They don't even have telephone lines modern enough for data links up there. It's the middle of nowhere."

"Then I'll make a satellite connection," she countered, opening cupboard doors and taking down bottles of formula and baby paraphernalia. She counted out a three-day supply and began packing it in her carry-on bag. She went to the refrigerator and took down the list she had made. Diapers. She was going to need another bag just for the diapers. She headed back into the bedroom.

Jonathan followed her.

"Will you stop," he said, taking her by the shoulder and forcibly pulling her to a

41

halt. He turned her around to face him.

Grace looked up into his usually affable, handsomely sculpted face. Only Jonathan wasn't looking so very agreeable now. He was angry. Truly angry. His intelligent, hazel-gray eyes were narrowed, and his jaw was clenched tightly enough to break his teeth.

Grace moved her gaze first to one of his hands on her arm and then to the other, noticing how his Rolex glistened beneath his perfectly pressed white cuff link shirt.

"You're hurting me," she said.

Ever a gentleman, even when angry, Jonathan immediately released her. He took a deep breath and stepped back, running his hand through his professionally styled sunblond hair.

"Dammit, Grace. This is the worst possible time for you to leave. We'll be receiving data from Podly by the end of the week."

And that was Jonathan's real worry. He wasn't disgruntled because he would miss her in a romantic sense, but because his business might suffer in her absence. The satellite pod they had sent up six weeks ago — it had been Grace's idea to name it Podly, because it reminded her of a long pea pod housing several delicate computers — was finally functioning to full capacity. And she was the only person at StarShip Spaceline who could decipher the data Podly sent back.

It was the race into space all over again, only this time it was not the Russians against the Americans. This new race involved private companies competing for the future market of civilian space travel. StarShip Spaceline was in a heated battle with two other private programs, one based in Europe, the other in Japan. And all three of them were on the verge of perfecting alternative forms of propulsion.

Solid rocket fuel, the propulsion used in the NASA space program, was inefficient. Simply put, it weighed too much. The shuttle had to be strapped to a rocket that was several times its size and weight just to get out of the Earth's atmosphere.

Alternative forms, such as ion propulsion or microwaves or antimatter, however, could make space travel a moneymaking venture and even make possible the colonization of the moon and Mars.

Basically, it all boiled down to mathematical physics.

And that was where Grace fit into the picture. She was StarShip Spaceline's resident mathematician. She crunched the numbers and was the troubleshooter for the theories. She could look at a schematic and tell, using mathematical formulas, if it was viable or not.

In just the eighteen months that she'd worked for StarShip, Grace had saved Jonathan Stanhope's company millions of dollars by disproving theories before they were put into action.

Podly was orbiting Earth right now, and there was great hope that the data it sent back would end the race for a new form of fuel in StarShip's favor.

"I can receive Podly's data in Maine just as well as I can here, Jonathan," she assured him. "I have the satellite link and my computer already packed."

"But what about your other projects?"

"Carl and Simon have been working on them these past four weeks without any problems. I see no reason why they can't continue."

She walked over to her closet and pulled down another bag to fill with diapers. She turned to find Jonathan blocking her path again. His features had softened, and his eyes were once again the intelligent hazel gray she had been falling in love with these past eighteen months.

"Grace. About the baby," he said softly.

"What about him?"

"Is he going to be with you when you return?"

Well now, that was the sixty-four-thousand-dollar question, wasn't it? Grace tried to remember which half-truths she had told Jonathan, as well as which lies she had told the social workers and her brothers. And what about the half-truths she had told Emma, the kindly nurse from the hospital who had been sympathetic enough to give up her vacation and help Grace with Baby these last four weeks?

"That's what I'm going to Maine to find out," she told Jonathan.

"The boy belongs with his father."

"He belongs with the person who can best care for him," she countered.

"You promised your sister," he reminded her. He took her by the shoulders again, but this time his touch was gentle. His expression, however, was not. "You're not dealing with Mary's death, Grace," he said, "because as long as you continue to hold on to her, you won't have to keep your promise."

"That's not true."

He reached up and pushed an unruly strand of hair from her face, tucking it behind her ear. "She's sitting in the middle of

45

your kitchen table right now. You've put your sister in an Oreo cookie tin, and you talk to her."

Grace stood her ground, refusing to let him see her pain. "She's my baby sister, Jonathan. You want me sticking her in a closet? Or maybe I should just FedEx her to Pine Creek? Mary loved Oreo cookies. I can't think of any place she'd rather be right now, until the Summer Solstice, when I'm supposed to put her to rest on TarStone Mountain."

"The Summer Solstice is four months away," he said, looking angry again. "I told you last week when you asked for this leave of absence that four months is too long. You've had one month already, and that's all I can spare right now."

"I'm taking four more months, Jonathan," she told him succinctly, bracing herself for a fight. "I owe that much to Mary and to Baby."

"You need to let go of her, Grace," he repeated, suddenly pulling her into his arms and hugging her tightly.

Grace sighed into his shoulder. She liked being in Jonathan's arms — usually. Heck, the few dates they'd been on had been showing great promise for a future together. Why, then, was she feeling disappointed? Could it be that this thoroughly modern, success-driven man she so admired didn't have a sensitive bone in his body? Could he really be this selfish, not to understand why she had to make things right with her sister?

"You need to go to Maine, find the kid's father, and move on with your life," he continued over her head. "Your sister has all but pulled you into the grave with her." He leaned back to see her. "Have you looked in the mirror lately? You're in jogging pants and a sweatshirt, for Christ's sake. The same ones you were wearing yesterday."

"They clean easier," she said, pulling away and stuffing the bag full of diapers. "Baby spit and formula do not go well with silk."

"And that's another thing," he continued to her back. "You're a scientist, not a mother. You don't know the first thing about raising a child. Hell, you can't even get the snaps on his suits right. The kid looks as disheveled as you do lately."

He took her by the shoulders again as soon as she turned to face him, making her drop the bag of diapers on the floor. "Grace," he whispered, his expression more desperate than angry. "Don't go. Not now. Wait until Podly lands in August, then go to Maine. It will be safer then."

"Safer?"

"It will be better," he amended. "Once the pod is safely landed and back in our hands, then you can leave."

"That's two months too late, Jonathan. I'll miss the Solstice. And I have to deal with Mary's estate. I can't just leave everything hanging for another six months. People in Pine Creek will wonder what happened to her."

"Call them," he said, squeezing her shoulders. "And call the kid's father and have him come get his son. It's the practical thing to do."

"For you," Grace hissed, pulling out of his grip and picking up the diaper bag. She straightened and glared at him. "You don't announce a person's death over the phone, and you sure as heck don't call a man and tell him the woman he loves is dead and 'oh, by the way, she left you a son.'"

Grace left the room before she brained her boss with the bag of diapers. She all but ran into the living room, only to stop at the sight of Emma feeding Baby.

Emma looked up and glared at a spot behind Grace, and Grace knew that Jonathan was standing behind her.

"I'll put your suitcase in my car," he said through gritted teeth. "Place whatever else you want to take by the door, and I'll get it."

"I'll put them in my car," she said, turning to face him. "Emma is driving Baby and me to the airport."

He ran a hand through his hair. "I guess I have no say in the matter," he said, his eyes still sharp with anger. "You know how much StarShip needs your expertise." His jaw tightened, and he pointed a finger at her. "I'll expect daily reports on Podly from you while you're gone — and it better not be for four months," he finished with a growl, just before he turned and silently walked out the door and headed for his car parked on the street.

"Now, don't you take anything he said to heart," Emma told her, admitting she had overheard their entire fight. "You're going to do just fine with this child, Grace. And as for your sister, I know what it's like to lose a loved one. You don't get over it in four weeks."

"Thank you, Emma. Ah, do you mind that I volunteered you to drive us to the airport? I just couldn't stand the thought of twenty more minutes of lectures from Jonathan."

"No, sweetie. It will be my pleasure. Here, he's ready for burping," she said, holding up Baby for Grace to take.

Gingerly, careful of the way she had been taught to support his head, Grace took Baby and turned him onto her shoulder. She patted his back with gentle, rhythmic strokes.

"Have you been thinking of a name?" Emma asked, packing Baby's clothes into yet another bag.

"I've thought of hundreds," Grace admitted, now pacing and patting and softly jouncing him up and down. "But none of them seems right," she said with averted eyes.

Lord, she hated lying to this nice lady. But she couldn't tell her she hadn't the right to christen Baby, that it was his father's privilege.

She had told the hospital staff and the social workers that she did not know who Baby's father was. It was the hardest lie she had ever told, but it was the most expedient — although it had been touch and go for a while. The hospital had been loath to release him without a Christian name to put on the birth certificate. As it stood, he was officially, temporarily, known as Baby Boy Sutter.

With only a bit of paperwork, and not liking the no-name situation any more than the hospital had, the courts had awarded Grace temporary custody of Baby until they could ask their counterparts in Maine to look into the matter. Upon hearing that news, Grace had even gone so far as to make up a tale that Mary had admitted having a one-night stand with a man who had been passing through Pine Creek. It was a wonder the cookie tin hadn't exploded all over her kitchen for that damning lie, but Grace had not wanted anyone investigating anything.

Her brothers were another matter altogether. Every one of them had promised to book a flight when Grace had called with the terrible news. But she convinced them there was nothing they could do here and that if they wished to express their love for Mary, they would show up at TarStone Mountain on the Summer Solstice.

Her lie to them had been one of omission. She had not told them about Baby.

Although Grace loved each of them dearly, she did not want them coming here and taking charge of a situation they knew nothing about. Not that she knew much more. But how could she explain she knew who the father was but that he thought he was a traveler through time? And how could she omit that little detail without first meeting Michael MacBain and deciding for herself if he was sane or not?

No, it was better this way. She didn't want or need six strong-minded men messing up the promise she had made to her sister.

Grace walked to the living-room window and saw Jonathan's Mercedes pull away from the stop sign at the end of her street. She buried her nose in Baby's hair, drawing in a long, satisfying whiff of shampoo and powder.

She had just had her first fight with Jonathan, and it had been an illuminating event.

He was worried about his company, the competition that was rapidly closing in on them, and Podly's performance. Well, she couldn't do anything about their competitors, but she could take care of Podly, even from Maine. Jonathan would calm down once he realized that he hadn't lost her expertise, only her physical presence. She would do a good job for StarShip these next four months and maybe set a precedent for an annual sabbatical in Maine.

But there had been something else in

Jonathan's voice and actions lately that simply didn't add up. If she had to put a name on it, Grace would call it fear. Jonathan had seemed scared just now that he couldn't talk her out of leaving.

Was he afraid she might not come back?

Or was the satellite his only concern?

Just before Podly had been launched six weeks ago, Jonathan had become quiet and withdrawn. He'd canceled a date with her at the last minute and had sequestered himself in the lab with Podly for nearly four days after that, placing the last bolt on the satellite himself, sealing it for its eight-month orbit around Earth.

And since it had been launched, Jonathan had been acting strangely with everyone at work. The first two weeks Podly had been up, before Mary's accident, Jonathan had spent every possible minute looking over Grace's shoulder at the computer bank that was the mission control for the small satellite — when, that is, he wasn't locked in his office with the blinds drawn. More than once Grace had come to work only to realize that Jonathan had never left.

He'd doubled security at the lab and threatened everyone to be on the alert for corporate espionage. Probably the only reason Grace wasn't as paranoid as Jonathan was because she had spent the last four weeks wrapped up in her own grief and Baby's care.

And that was another thing.

Jonathan didn't want Baby. He expected her to make a phone call, hand Baby over to a stranger, then get on with business as usual.

The subject of children had come up once on a date, and Jonathan had casually alluded to the fact that they would make quite a baby together, that their child would have a genetic makeup that could not help but ensure great intelligence.

At the time Grace had been thrilled that Jonathan was even thinking such thoughts about their future together. Now, though, she was beginning to wonder if the man was dating her for who she was or for the genes she was carrying. He might be open to the idea of having his own carefully engineered baby, but he definitely wanted nothing to do with another man's child.

That was something else she would have to think about these next four months.

"He's spit up on you again," Emma said, breaking into Grace's thoughts. "It's running down the back of your shoulder."

Emma tossed a towel over Grace's shoulder and took Baby away from her.

"You've got to be more gentle with the tyke, Grace," she said, smiling as she gave her critique. "Handle him the way you handle your laptop computer. Hold him firmly, but don't jostle him too much."

Grace wiped the spit from her shirt and flopped down into a chair. She threw the towel across the room, aiming for the dirty clothes basket. She missed. "I'm never going to make it as a mother, Emma. I can't seem to get the hang of it."

Grace blew the hair from her cheek and reached up and tucked it behind her ear. "I have all the confidence a person could want when it comes to splitting atoms or launching rockets into space." She waved at Baby. "But I can't even dress him without having snaps left over when I get to his neck. And the sticky tape on his diapers defeats me. He comes away naked when I pull off his jumpsuits."

Emma was truly laughing now as she set Baby down and started changing him into his traveling clothes. Grace got up from her chair and moved closer to watch.

"You're sure he's not too young to travel?" she asked over Emma's shoulder, fascinated by the woman's effortless skill.

"Naw. He's as strong as an ox, this one. And the doctor gave you permission." She

55

looked up at Grace. "Believe me, Dr. Brown would not have let him go if he had any doubts. Here. You rock him to sleep, and I'll finish packing his things." She walked to where she'd set down her purse and pulled out a book. "Where's your carry-on?" she asked. "I brought you some reading for the flight."

"What is it?" Grace asked.

"It's a book on babies," Emma said, holding it up for Grace to see. "Written by two women who know what they're doing. Between them, they've got eight children." She tucked the book into the bag by the hall doorway.

"You're sending me off with an owner's manual?" Grace asked, her laugh getting stuck on the lump in her throat.

Emma straightened and looked Grace in the eye. "You go with your instincts first, Grace. If you think something's wrong, get Baby to a doctor. But usually just common sense will see you through each day. And if in doubt, check this book or call me." She pulled a piece of paper from her pocket and tucked it into the bag beside the book. "These are my numbers, for home and work. You call."

Grace tamped down the tears threatening to blur her vision. She had known

Emma only four weeks, and already the woman was as much a mother as she'd had in more than nine years.

"Thank you, Emma. For everything," Grace whispered hoarsely.

Emma looked at her watch, ducking her head. But not before Grace saw a flush creep into the woman's face.

"I'll take this out to your car and check the car seat," Emma said, her voice gruff as she picked up the bag. "You'll miss your flight if we don't get going."

Grace rocked her nephew, tempted to close her eyes and fall asleep with him. What was she doing, taking him on such a journey at such a young age? Three flights, each plane decidedly smaller than the previous one. A jet from Virginia to Boston, a turbo-prop from Boston to Bangor, Maine, and then a six-seat bush plane that probably had skis instead of wheels for the last leg from Bangor to home.

What was she hoping to find in Pine Creek?

And just how many more lies would she have to tell before Mary's ghost rose up from her ashes and bit her on the backside?

Chapter Three

The first thing he noticed was the baby strapped to her chest. The second thing was the fact that she wasn't wearing a wedding band.

That first little detail should have made the second one moot, but Greylen MacKeage had never been one to run from a fight or from babies. Nor was he prone to second-guessing his gut. Not when his reaction to a woman was this strong.

The hair on the back of his neck stirred when she walked toward him in the Bangor airport terminal looking lost and tired and in desperate need of assistance. But it wasn't until she walked up to the pilot holding the "Sutter" sign that his senses sharpened acutely.

They would be sharing the plane to Pine Creek.

Which was a blessing for Grey. He needed the distraction of a beautiful woman to take his mind off the fact that he would soon be three thousand feet up in the sky with nothing but air between him and the ground. He couldn't decide which was worse, the three thousand feet for the next leg of his ride from Bangor to Pine Creek or the thirty thousand feet he had flown at coming from Chicago. Not that it mattered. From either height, the ground was just as hard when you fell.

"You're Grace Sutter?" the impatient pilot asked when she stopped in front of him and carefully set down her bags.

She nodded.

"You related to Mary Sutter?"

She nodded again.

Just as impatient to get this flight over with as the pilot seemed to be, Grey silently folded the newspaper he'd been reading and studied Grace Sutter. He knew Mary, too.

"You don't look like your sister," the pilot said, giving her a skeptical once-over, as if he didn't believe her.

Grey did. This woman looked a bit older than Mary, but then that might just be the state of exhaustion she was obviously in. Her soft-looking, tousled blond hair was longer, lighter, and a tad more wild. The cherub shape of her face and the cant of her chin were identical to her sister's, and she was shorter than Mary by a good three inches. And her eyes? Well, they were a deeper, more liquid blue, set off by flawless skin the color of newly fallen snow. But stand the sisters side by side, and a blind man could see the resemblance.

He hoped like hell their pilot wasn't blind.

Grey knew Mary Sutter as a neighbor. She owned a small herb farm on the west side of his mountain. The same farm he had unsuccessfully been trying to buy for the last two years. The MacKeages owned nearly four hundred thousand acres of prime Maine forest, and the Sutter land sat right in the corner of a very nice piece of it.

For two years Mary had sold him eggs, herbs, even goat cheese, but she would not sell him her home.

Grey hadn't pushed the issue. He didn't really need her sixty-one acres, he just wanted to neaten up his western boundary. But all he had been able to get from Mary, other than food, was the promise that if she ever decided to sell, she'd sell to him.

And so Grey had remained content to be good neighbors. When Mary's roof had needed repair, he'd sent Morgan and Callum over to fix it. Not that she had asked for his help.

Mary Sutter was an independent woman. And that had been fine with Grey, until he had caught her thirty feet up on the roof one day, with one end of a rope tied around her waist and the other end tied to the chimney. He had decided then that independence in a woman was a dangerous thing.

He had made the foolish mistake of telling her so.

Mary had laughed in his face.

But she had accepted his offer to help. Mary Sutter may be independent, but she wasn't stupid. She didn't like heights any more than he did.

Grey had asked her out once. So had Morgan and Callum and even too-old-for-her Ian. She had kindly, gracefully, refused them all. And then the crazy woman had been seen all over town with the bastard MacBain.

Go figure.

"I know Mary," the pilot said. He looked around the terminal and then at a piece of paper he held with his sign. "I don't have her listed for this trip." He looked at Grace Sutter. "She's not home, you know. Been gone about five months."

"I know," Grace Sutter said softly.

The baby that was snuggled deeply in

the sack on her chest suddenly stirred. The pilot took a step back, not having realized the woman had a child with her.

Dammit. He *was* blind.

Grey was seriously thinking of renting a car for the last ninety miles of his journey. But the rental company insisted he return the damn thing back here; they had no outlets in the middle of the woods. So that wasn't an option. Neither was calling one of his men to come get him. They were too close to the scheduled opening of the resort, and they were nowhere near ready.

Grey stood up, slung his bag over his shoulder, and stooped to pick up Grace Sutter's two bags by her feet. He was surprised by the weight of one of them. He was even more surprised when she grabbed the lightest one back from him.

He lifted his head to find himself staring over a baby's head into the deep blue eyes of the woman he intended to marry.

Grey straightened as if he'd been punched. What in hell was this all about? He suddenly felt too big for his skin, his knees wanted to buckle, and he couldn't seem to catch his breath.

"Ah . . . I'll hold on to this one, thank you," she said, her voice barely penetrating the haze in his head. He saw her turn to

as nothing to worry
th the blizzards he'd
t great unending land

been impressed. He
the Beaver and stowed
Sutter's heavy suitcase
looked around the
rs, and his stomach
ad offered him a seat up
ad declined. He'd take the
, where he wouldn't feel
atch every gauge on the
f trouble.

Grace Sutter said from be-
e rain is starting to freeze.
rried about icing?"

ady seemed to know a bit
Grey's spirits rose.

Mark said, giving her a look
clear he hadn't liked the ques-
warmer aloft. The cold air's
nder two thousand feet."

landing strip near Pine Creek
hundred," she said then. "And
thousand-foot ceiling is prob-
three thousand feet in the moun-
e're going to be descending
twenty-two hundred feet of
rain."

the pilot. "I have three more bags and a car seat waiting at the luggage counter."

Grey turned and walked out the side door of the terminal without looking back. The cold, drizzling February rain hit him full on the face. He stood there, his head lifted to the sky, and let the rain wash all the fog from his brain.

Talk about reactions. The lady was beautiful enough to take any man's breath away, but marriage?

Grey shook his head, disgusted with himself. Granted, he did have marriage on his mind lately, but he was expecting the courtship to last a bit longer than two seconds. Yes, that was what had struck him a moment ago — his body was already looking for a mate even if his brain had not caught up to it yet.

Yeah. That's what happened. A beautiful woman had simply stepped in front of a man on the hunt.

Grey had called a clan meeting just a few weeks ago to discuss this very subject. It was time, he had told his men, that they all got married. They had their land, the resort was due to open next month, and it was time they looked to the future. They needed sons. Lots of sons, with whom they could start building the MacKeage clan back to the greatness it once was.

His men had not embraced the idea. They were still trying to cope with the fact that they were no longer warriors, which was an honorable profession in their minds, but merchants, which was not. They were selling pleasure and sport to hordes of vacationers who traveled from the overcrowded cities of the south.

And wives? Why would they want to go and add to their troubles? Wives would mean separate households, regular haircuts, and going to church.

Getting married would also mean having to mingle with the moderns to find those wives in the first place. Courting meant dating now, going to restaurants, dances, and movie theaters where a bunch of people sat in the dark and were nearly bowled over by noisy stories acted out on a screen.

Courting also meant getting involved with the women's families, and it was the consensus of the men that most families today were downright odd. Half the people in this world were divorced, and the rest were on their second, third, and sometimes fourth marriages. People swapped spouses today more often than they had swapped horses eight hundred years ago.

No. No
get marri
But Gre
nancial po
sons to ens
generation w
the land, th
power that ca
clan MacKeage

Several pellet
mixed with the
Grey shrugged hi
and began walking

It was a six-seat
had flown in one lik
ders, all of them exp
and an oil filler pipe

Not a reassuring pic

Damn, he hated smal
an unnatural act. It def
that tons of steel could
means of a little stick bo
spinning around and arou
wind.

But more than he hated
Grey really hated overcon
While waiting for Grace Sut
the pilot — who had introduc
Mark — had bragged about hi
misses as a bush pilot up in Al

the pilot. "I have three more bags and a car seat waiting at the luggage counter."

Grey turned and walked out the side door of the terminal without looking back. The cold, drizzling February rain hit him full on the face. He stood there, his head lifted to the sky, and let the rain wash all the fog from his brain.

Talk about reactions. The lady was beautiful enough to take any man's breath away, but marriage?

Grey shook his head, disgusted with himself. Granted, he did have marriage on his mind lately, but he was expecting the courtship to last a bit longer than two seconds. Yes, that was what had struck him a moment ago — his body was already looking for a mate even if his brain had not caught up to it yet.

Yeah. That's what happened. A beautiful woman had simply stepped in front of a man on the hunt.

Grey had called a clan meeting just a few weeks ago to discuss this very subject. It was time, he had told his men, that they all got married. They had their land, the resort was due to open next month, and it was time they looked to the future. They needed sons. Lots of sons, with whom they could start building the MacKeage clan back to the greatness it once was.

His men had not embraced the idea. They were still trying to cope with the fact that they were no longer warriors, which was an honorable profession in their minds, but merchants, which was not. They were selling pleasure and sport to hordes of vacationers who traveled from the overcrowded cities of the south.

And wives? Why would they want to go and add to their troubles? Wives would mean separate households, regular haircuts, and going to church.

Getting married would also mean having to mingle with the moderns to find those wives in the first place. Courting meant dating now, going to restaurants, dances, and movie theaters where a bunch of people sat in the dark and were nearly bowled over by noisy stories acted out on a screen.

Courting also meant getting involved with the women's families, and it was the consensus of the men that most families today were downright odd. Half the people in this world were divorced, and the rest were on their second, third, and sometimes fourth marriages. People swapped spouses today more often than they had swapped horses eight hundred years ago.

No. None of his men was in any hurry to get married.

But Grey was adamant. They had the financial power base now, and they needed sons to ensure its continuance. The next generation would be businessmen, utilizing the land, the timber, and the political power that came with both. The future of clan MacKeage lay in their children.

Several pellets of ice struck his face, mixed with the cold, heavily misting rain. Grey shrugged his collar closer to his neck and began walking toward the plane.

It was a six-seat DeHaviland Beaver. He had flown in one like it before. Nine cylinders, all of them exposed to the weather, and an oil filler pipe in the cockpit.

Not a reassuring picture.

Damn, he hated small planes. Flying was an unnatural act. It defied common sense that tons of steel could lift into the air by means of a little stick bolted to the nose, spinning around and around to stir up the wind.

But more than he hated small planes, Grey really hated overconfident pilots. While waiting for Grace Sutter to arrive, the pilot — who had introduced himself as Mark — had bragged about his many near misses as a bush pilot up in Alaska. That a little winter rain was nothing to worry about, compared with the blizzards he'd flown through in that great unending land of snow and ice.

Grey had not been impressed. He opened the door of the Beaver and stowed his bag and Grace Sutter's heavy suitcase in the back. He looked around the cramped quarters, and his stomach churned. Mark had offered him a seat up front, but Grey had declined. He'd take the back, thank you, where he wouldn't feel compelled to watch every gauge on the dash for signs of trouble.

"Ah, Mark?" Grace Sutter said from behind him. "The rain is starting to freeze. You're not worried about icing?"

Well, the lady seemed to know a bit about flying. Grey's spirits rose.

"Nope," Mark said, giving her a look that made it clear he hadn't liked the question. "It's warmer aloft. The cold air's locked in under two thousand feet."

"But the landing strip near Pine Creek is at eight hundred," she said then. "And that two-thousand-foot ceiling is probably at three thousand feet in the mountains. We're going to be descending through twenty-two hundred feet of freezing rain."

"You a pilot?" Mark asked, sounding annoyed.

"No."

"Well, lady, I am. And I've flown in every type of weather on this planet. I'm telling you, it's safe to take off. I've checked the radar, and the rain stops twenty miles short of Pine Creek. It won't be a problem."

He cocked his head and shifted his stance, letting them know his patience was drawing to an end. "They're predicting this storm to settle in for several days. So it's either fly out now or be stuck here. It's your call, lady."

Grey watched Grace Sutter look down at the sleeping child on her chest. She looked around the tarmac and held up her hand, letting the freezing rain fall into her palm. She lifted it, watching it melt, and then she looked at Grey.

"Which seat do you want?" she asked then. "Or are you sitting up front in the copilot seat?"

"I'll take the middle," he told her, thankful that whatever had struck him inside the terminal was over. He still wanted the woman to the very soles of his feet, but his mind was once again in control of his body. "Why don't you sit beside me, and we'll make a bed in the backseat for your child?"

Her eyes widened, and Grey didn't know if he'd just scared her spitless or made her own toes tingle. He hoped it was the latter. And he hoped she would be staying in Pine Creek long enough for him to find out what she was doing running around with a bairn and no husband.

"Unless you want to sit up front," he said.

"Ah . . . no. The middle is fine."

Mark looked relieved. He opened the baggage door in the rear and stowed her three other suitcases and a child-carrier seat. Grey reached to take the bag she was holding. She clutched it to her side for a moment, then reluctantly let it go.

"Please be careful with that. And could you set it on the floor by my seat?" she asked.

"Let's load up, people," Mark said, climbing into the front of the plane.

Grey helped Grace Sutter aboard, then took the seat beside her. He handed her the side of her seat belt closer to him. She snapped it closed over her lap and under her child. Then she carefully pulled off her baby's cap.

A full head of dark, spike-straight hair

appeared, with two little ears sticking through it. Grey watched as Grace leaned down and kissed the sleeping baby on the top of his head.

"Is it a boy or a girl?" he asked, only to flinch at the sound of the engine sputtering to life.

"A boy."

"How old is he?"

"Four weeks."

Grey's gaze went from the child to her face. Four weeks? He was lusting after a woman barely out of childbed?

He studied her face. She might be tired and a bit frayed around the edges, but Grace Sutter didn't look like a woman who had spent the last nine months being pregnant. There was a special . . . presence new mothers possessed, and he was not seeing it now as he studied her.

"Is he yours?" he asked without thinking.

She turned and gave him an icy glare.

"I'm sorry. That was rude of me," he quickly amended. "It's just that you look too good to have a four-week-old son."

He watched a flush creep into her cheeks. Great. Maybe his brain really wasn't in charge of his mouth at the moment.

"Look," he said with a sigh. "Can we start over? I'm Greylen MacKeage," he said, holding out his hand for her to take. "And I know your sister. We're neighbors."

"MacKeage," she repeated, staring at his hand, looking as if she was afraid it would bite her.

After a moment she accepted his peace offering and put her small hand into his. He just as carefully closed his fingers around hers and shook it, instantly aware of a warm, unsettling tingle that traveled up his arm.

"I'm Grace Sutter," she said, pulling back her hand. Grey noticed that she clenched that hand into a fist just before she tucked it under her thigh.

"Mary mentioned the MacKeages," she said then. "Don't you own TarStone Mountain?"

"That's right."

"You're building a ski resort and summer spa," she said, not as a question but as a statement of fact. "Mary mentioned that it's due to open soon."

"In about a month," he told her. Maybe they weren't off to such a bad start.

Her face lit up with a smile. "That should help out the economy of Pine Creek."

They still had a hard time compre-
ing a world full of so many different
le, where courts of law settled dis-
s and where marriages simply ended
women were left to bring up families
hemselves.

ut not six months into their painstaking
ons, Daar began to insist that it would
wise for them to leave Scotland. That
ving to a more remote, less populated
d — such as the northeastern forests of
United States, maybe — might make
ir lives easier. But before he could con-
ce them that America was where they
ould go, Grey made the priest take him
the site of their old keep. There was a
hoolhouse there now, and the name
lacKeage was scattered to all four corners
f modern-day Scotland.

And so Grey had agreed to leave.

Michael MacBain and his five men had
ept themselves separate as much as was
possible, and when the time came for them
to go out on their own, he took his men to
Nova Scotia.

Daar had sold a couple of their saddles,
now valuable antiques, and presented them
with bundles of paper money to finance
the trip. But it had been Callum's and
Ian's swords and Grey's jeweled dagger

"Not everyone thinks we're doing a good
thing," he admitted with a sheepish grin.
"People are afraid the town will lose its
identity."

She thought about that. "Maybe," she
said, her hand absently petting down her
son's hair. "But it survived the boom and
then the decline of the logging era. I think
it can survive your resort. I bet you a
penny the locals will be the first to open up
shops and hang out shingles to sell maple
syrup, hand-knit sweaters, and bed-and-
breakfast rooms."

"You'd probably double your money," he
agreed.

"You all buckled up back there?" Mark
asked, moving the plane toward the
runway.

Grey turned to Grace. "You want to
keep your son in his cocoon? Or would you
like me to set up his car seat in the back?"

She patted her baby's bottom affectionately. "No, but thank you. He's sleeping
now. I think I'll just let him be."

Grey turned toward his window then, so
Grace Sutter couldn't see his face when
the plane lifted off the tarmac. He gripped
the seat with one hand and the door
handle with the other, closed his eyes, and
started his usual litany of prayers.

They were the same prayers he used late at night, when he was alone in his bed and felt he had lost his mind. Although he would wake up from the nightmares — where he relived the horror of the great storm, the lightning, and the terror — Grey still found himself in a strange new land where metal machines raced by at unbelievable speeds, where light appeared in a room like magic, and where hordes of people seemed to be everywhere.

At first, Grey and his men and the six bastard MacBains had honestly thought they had died and been condemned to hell. They had survived the storm only to be nearly killed by what they had thought were speeding demons but now knew were automobiles. The sheep and cattle in the pastures they recognized. The people in those automobiles, dressed so strangely, they did not. They had seen the steeple of a large stone church in the distance and had hidden in an abandoned barn until dark before they made their way to it, hoping to find sanctuary there.

They'd found Father Daar instead.

The old priest had been at the altar praying when the ten of them had walked inside, leading their warhorses into the church with them, not caring anymore what God might think of su...

Daar had calmly turned ar... comed them into God's hous... calmly listened to their stor... keeled over dead or run away... which was suspect in itsel... thinking. How balanced cou... mind be, no matter how brittle... stand bravely before ten d... scared warriors, smiling and n... they all rushed to tell him their in...

But Daar had not only unders... language, he spoke it himself, ma... calm their fears even though he... explain what had happened any m... they could.

Over the next nine months the ol... had patiently and steadfastly given... the tools they needed to survive... twenty-first century. Daar had taugh... the modern language, about mone... commerce, as well as manners and th... of eating utensils. He had ruthl... pushed them to drive vehicles and sho... them the wondrous technologies avail... today. And the displaced warriors had... luctantly but quickly adapted to the n... world they found themselves in now.

It had not been easy. In fact, it was st... not easy for any of them. They were wa...

"Not everyone thinks we're doing a good thing," he admitted with a sheepish grin. "People are afraid the town will lose its identity."

She thought about that. "Maybe," she said, her hand absently petting down her son's hair. "But it survived the boom and then the decline of the logging era. I think it can survive your resort. I bet you a penny the locals will be the first to open up shops and hang out shingles to sell maple syrup, hand-knit sweaters, and bed-and-breakfast rooms."

"You'd probably double your money," he agreed.

"You all buckled up back there?" Mark asked, moving the plane toward the runway.

Grey turned to Grace. "You want to keep your son in his cocoon? Or would you like me to set up his car seat in the back?"

She patted her baby's bottom affectionately. "No, but thank you. He's sleeping now. I think I'll just let him be."

Grey turned toward his window then, so Grace Sutter couldn't see his face when the plane lifted off the tarmac. He gripped the seat with one hand and the door handle with the other, closed his eyes, and started his usual litany of prayers.

They were the same prayers he used late at night, when he was alone in his bed and felt he had lost his mind. Although he would wake up from the nightmares — where he relived the horror of the great storm, the lightning, and the terror — Grey still found himself in a strange new land where metal machines raced by at unbelievable speeds, where light appeared in a room like magic, and where hordes of people seemed to be everywhere.

At first, Grey and his men and the six bastard MacBains had honestly thought they had died and been condemned to hell. They had survived the storm only to be nearly killed by what they had thought were speeding demons but now knew were automobiles. The sheep and cattle in the pastures they recognized. The people in those automobiles, dressed so strangely, they did not. They had seen the steeple of a large stone church in the distance and had hidden in an abandoned barn until dark before they made their way to it, hoping to find sanctuary there.

They'd found Father Daar instead.

The old priest had been at the altar praying when the ten of them had walked inside, leading their warhorses into the church with them, not caring anymore what God might think of such an act.

Daar had calmly turned around and welcomed them into God's house and just as calmly listened to their story. He hadn't keeled over dead or run away screaming — which was suspect in itself to Grey's thinking. How balanced could a man's mind be, no matter how brittle with age, to stand bravely before ten dangerously scared warriors, smiling and nodding as they all rushed to tell him their insane tale.

But Daar had not only understood their language, he spoke it himself, managing to calm their fears even though he couldn't explain what had happened any more than they could.

Over the next nine months the old priest had patiently and steadfastly given them the tools they needed to survive in this twenty-first century. Daar had taught them the modern language, about money and commerce, as well as manners and the use of eating utensils. He had ruthlessly pushed them to drive vehicles and showed them the wondrous technologies available today. And the displaced warriors had reluctantly but quickly adapted to the new world they found themselves in now.

It had not been easy. In fact, it was still not easy for any of them. They were warriors. They still had a hard time comprehending a world full of so many different people, where courts of law settled disputes and where marriages simply ended and women were left to bring up families by themselves.

But not six months into their painstaking lessons, Daar began to insist that it would be wise for them to leave Scotland. That moving to a more remote, less populated land — such as the northeastern forests of the United States, maybe — might make their lives easier. But before he could convince them that America was where they should go, Grey made the priest take him to the site of their old keep. There was a schoolhouse there now, and the name MacKeage was scattered to all four corners of modern-day Scotland.

And so Grey had agreed to leave.

Michael MacBain and his five men had kept themselves separate as much as was possible, and when the time came for them to go out on their own, he took his men to Nova Scotia.

Daar had sold a couple of their saddles, now valuable antiques, and presented them with bundles of paper money to finance the trip. But it had been Callum's and Ian's swords and Grey's jeweled dagger